With Love to
All Our Own Special Bunnies,
Big and Small

Random House 🏠 New York

Conceived and developed by Nancy Bracken Garson and Tom Garson, with art direction by Linda Haase Kane.

Copyright © 2009 by Lovable Products International, Inc.

Visit us on the Web! www.randomhouse.com/kids

Educators and librarians, for a variety of teaching tools, visit us at www.randomhouse.com/teachers

Library of Congress Cataloging-in-Publication Data
Yeh, Kat.
You're lovable to me / by Kat Yeh ; illustrated by Sue Anderson. —
1st ed.   p.   cm.
Summary: After Mama puts her bunnies to bed with words of love,
Grandpa delivers the same reassuring message to his sleeping daughter.
ISBN 978-0-375-86015-7 (trade) — ISBN 978-0-375-96015-4 (lib. bdg.)
[1. Mother and child—Fiction.   2. Parent and child—Fiction.   3. Love—Fiction.
4. Bedtime—Fiction.   5. Rabbits—Fiction.]   I. Anderson, Sue, ill.   II. Title.
PZ7.Y3658Wh 2010   [E]—dc22   2008037546

MANUFACTURED IN CHINA   10 9 8 7 6 5 4 3 2 1   First Edition

You're
Lovable to Me

By Kat Yeh

Illustrated by Sue Anderson

It had been a big day.

It had been a hard night.

"We're sorry!" sniffed the bunnies
as Mama turned down the light.

Mama smiled softly,
and she drew them to her knee.

"Bunnies, let me tell you something
someone used to say to me. . . .

When a mama loves a bunny,
she will love him when he's sad

or he's frightened

or she's lonely

or he's worried

or she's mad

or when he's plain exhausted

or embarrassed

or just shy

or when they have the giggles

and can't stop to tell you why.

No matter what your feelings are,
whatever they may be . . .

I'm your mama.
You're my bunnies.

And you're lovable to me."

It had been a big day.

It had been a hard night.

When Grandpa came for evening tea,
he found a sleepy sight.

He smiled and got a blanket
and kissed Mama on the head.

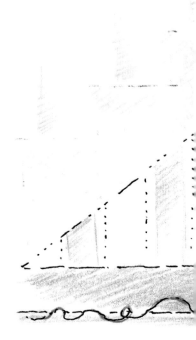

He looked at her a long, long time,
and this is what he said. . . .

"**W**hen a papa loves a bunny,
he still loves her when she's grown . . .

with a home that's filled with love and hope
and bunnies of her own.

When a papa loves a bunny,
that's the way it will always be.

I'm your papa.
You're still my bunny.

And you're lovable to me."

Good night,
my little bunny.